The Bridesmaid Ballet

The Bridesmaid Ballet

Katharine Holabird
Illustrated by Chris Russell
Based on the original drawings by Helen Craig

PUFFIN

To my lovely nieces, Melinda, Olivia and Emma
— with tons of love

PUFFIN BOOKS

Published by the Penguin Group
Penguin Books Ltd, 80 Strand, London WC2R 0RL, England
Penguin Group (USA) Inc., 375 Hudson Street, New York, New York 10014, USA
Penguin Group (Canada), 90 Eglinton Avenue East, Suite 700, Toronto, Ontario, Canada M4P 2Y3
(a division of Pearson Penguin Canada Inc.)
Penguin Ireland, 25 St Stephen's Green, Dublin 2, Ireland (a division of Penguin Books Ltd)
Penguin Group (Australia), 250 Camberwell Road, Camberwell, Victoria 3124, Australia
(a division of Pearson Australia Group Pty Ltd)
Penguin Books India Pvt Ltd, 11 Community Centre, Panchsheel Park, New Delhi – 110 017, India
Penguin Group (NZ), 67 Apollo Drive, Mairangi Bay, Auckland 1310, New Zealand
(a division of Pearson New Zealand Ltd)
Penguin Books (South Africa) (Pty) Ltd, 24 Sturdee Avenue, Rosebank, Johannesburg 2196, South Africa

Penguin Books Ltd, Registered Offices: 80 Strand, London WC2R 0RL, England

penguin.com

Published 2006
2

Copyright © HIT Entertainment Limited, 2006
Text copyright © Katharine Holabird, 2006
Illustrations copyright © Chris Russell, 2006
Illustrations based on the original drawings by Helen Craig © Helen Craig, 2006
All rights reserved

The moral right of the author and illustrator has been asserted

Angelina, Angelina Ballerina and the Dancing Angelina logo are trademarks of HIT Entertainment Limited,
Katharine Holabird and Helen Craig Ltd. Angelina is registered in the UK, Japan, and US Pat. & TM. Off.
The Dancing Angelina logo is registered in the UK.

Typeset in Comic Sans MS by Palimpsest Book Production Limited, Polmont, Stirlingshire
Made and printed in England by Clays Ltd, St Ives plc

Except in the United States of America, this book is sold subject to the condition that it shall not, by
way of trade or otherwise, be lent, re-sold, hired out, or otherwise circulated without the publisher's
prior consent in any form of binding or cover other than that in which it is published and without a
similar condition including this condition being imposed on the subsequent purchaser

British Library Cataloguing in Publication Data
A CIP catalogue record for this book is available from the British Library

ISBN-13: 978-0-141-32125-7
ISBN-10: 0-141-32125-3

To find out more about Angelina, visit her website at **www.angelinaballerina.com**

The Bridesmaid Ballet

Dear Diary

I have a truly ginormous wish – I would soooo LOVE to be a bridesmaid! I can't wait to be invited to a gorgeous wedding . . . I'll need a special bridesmaid dress and shiny ribbons and dancing slippers and a wreath of flowers in my fur. Imagine!

My very bestest friend Alice agrees

1

with me. She says that bridesmaids are the best thing since Cheddar cheese!

After school today Alice and I skipped home to Honeysuckle Cottage together, and clambered up the old oak tree at the bottom of my garden. Alice was giggling with excitement as I opened the creaky door of our Treetop Club.

'So what's the big surprise, Angelina?' she asked, as we plopped down on our comfy cushions. I poured two glasses of pink lemonade and opened a bag of cheesy niblets.

'Here it is!' I shouted. Then I pulled
out my fantabulous new poster and
showed it to her.

'Oooh – it's Serena Silvertail in the
Cindermouse ballet,' said Alice, admiring
the famous ballerina. 'She's soooo
beautiful!'

'I specially sent away for it,' I said
proudly, 'to decorate our clubhouse.'

I tacked the poster up on the wall and
Alice and I gazed at it.

'She's waltzing with Prince Charming at the royal wedding,' I explained.

'Her dress is truly sparkly,' Alice whispered dreamily, 'and so is her silvery tiara.'

'Don't you wish we could go to Cindermouse's wedding?' I asked, examining my old dress. 'And be the bridesmaids?'

'With special fancy dresses!' said Alice.

'And fancy slippers too!' I added.

'Aaah,' Alice and I sighed together and closed our eyes. Imagine!

Dear Diary

This morning I was so cosy in my bed I didn't even wake up for breakfast. In my dreams I was dancing gracefully behind a beautiful bride and holding her lacy veil as she waltzed through a garden of roses.

I knew I'd seen the bride before, but I just couldn't remember her name. It didn't really matter though, because I was definitely the prettiest bridesmaid ever!

'Thank you, Angelina,' whispered the bride. 'You're my most very special bridesmaid.'

'OUCH!' I yelped.

I woke up with a start. My baby sister, Polly, was thumping me with her grubby paws. Grrrr . . . (Polly is definitely the worst pest ever.)

'Can't you see I'm busy dreaming?' I asked. I yanked the pillow over my head and tried to snuggle back under the covers.

'Yummy pancakes!' Polly shrieked, bouncing on the bed. The scrumptious smell of Mum's blueberry pancakes wafted upstairs. My tummy rumbled in a very unbridesmaidlike way and my dream rose garden disappeared. I leapt out of bed and raced down the stairs before my silly little sister could gobble up all the pancakes (she is soooo greedy!).

'Good morning, girls,' said Mum, as Polly and I dashed madly into the kitchen. Mum heaped three humongous pancakes on my plate. Yum!

'Your mother's the best cook ever,' said Dad, sitting down with a smile.

'Definitely,' I agreed. My whiskers were twitching to ask Mum a big question.

'Mum, please tell me tons more about your wedding,' I said. 'Was it the very bestest day of your life?'

Mum smiled. 'Your father was as handsome as a prince, but I was so nervous I forgot my bridal bouquet,' she said, sipping her coffee. 'Luckily, your Aunt Lavender was my bridesmaid. She found the bouquet and saved the day.'

Dad chuckled. 'And then your handsome prince tripped over the door of the church and bumped his head,' he said.

How gruesome!

'Did Aunt Lavender have a special dress?' I asked.

'The loveliest bridesmaid dress I ever saw,' said Mum, pointing to the big wedding photo on the shelf. I stood on my tippy-toes (I'm soooo good at tippy-toes because of all my ballet lessons) and admired Aunt Lavender's sparkly bridesmaid dress – it was really-truly gorgeous.

'Oh, I hope hope hope I get to be a
bridesmaid some day!' I sighed, gobbling
the last pancake.

Miss Lilly was most definitely unfair at
ballet school today. I was twirling in my
ballet slippers, just like Cindermouse at
the royal wedding, when I made a totally
tiny mistake and squished William's tail . . .

'YOWEEE!' shouted William.

'Pay attention, Angelina,' scolded Miss
Lilly. 'No daydreaming in class.'

'Yes, Miss Lilly,' I answered, my tail
drooping. After that, I swirled and
twirled around the room very carefully,
because Miss Lilly says ballerinas should

ALWAYS be disciplined (and that means not twirling on other mouselings' tails). But while I was gracefully pirouetting just like Cindermouse's most favourite bridesmaid, my annoying little cousin Henry hopped in front of me and I bumped into him.

Oomph. 'Be careful, Henry!' I shouted.

'Mouselings must dance gracefully, my darlinks,' Miss Lilly reminded us (Miss Lilly always calls us her darlinks).

'ANGELINA SQUASHED ME,' Henry complained.

'I'll have a chat with Angelina after our lesson,' said Miss Lilly, while the horrid Pinkpaws twins sniggered and pointed at me. (Ugh. They are soooo rude!)

'Angelina, darlink,' said Miss Lilly, when everyone had left, 'is there a problem?'

'No, Miss Lilly,' I said, 'but . . .'

'But what, my little mouseling?' asked Miss Lilly.

'Well, I've been dreaming about being a dancing bridesmaid in a sparkly dress, with flowers and ribbons and everything . . .'

I stopped. Miss Lilly's whiskers definitely seemed to be twitching and suddenly a question popped right into my head.

'Have you ever thought about getting married, Miss Lilly?' I asked.

'Goodness gracious, no!' exclaimed Miss Lilly, shaking her head. 'You see, I never found the perfect partner, Angelina.'

Dear Diary

'What do you think, Alice?' I asked, as we climbed up into the Treetop Club with our yummy snacks after ballet school. 'Will Miss Lilly ever find the perfect partner?'

'Well, she is a bit old . . .' said Alice thoughtfully, putting down her satchel and munching a handful of cheesy pops (you have to be careful or Alice will eat them ALL!).

'But Miss Lilly could still fall in love!' I protested. Then I had the most brilliant idea ever! 'Oooh! We can help her to find someone – like a handsome old ballet star.'

'But there aren't even any handsome young ballet stars in Chipping Cheddar,' Alice objected, rolling her eyes. 'Any more cheesy pops?'

Humph! I thought that was a truly tippety-top idea . . .

'Imagine, Alice – you'll get married some day,' I teased, passing her the very last cheesy pop (honestly!). 'You'll look soooo gorgeous in your fancy wedding dress kissing the groom.'

'NO WAY!' shrieked Alice, sticking out her tongue. 'Anyhow, you're going to marry William Longtail,' she said. 'I know because he told me so.'

'Horrors!' I screamed, and we both collapsed in a complete fit of the giggles.

Dear Diary

I've been keeping an eye on Miss Lilly lately because she's acting very weird. At ballet class she lost all the sheet music, and I had to climb under the piano (ugh – it was soooo dusty!) and poke around in the lockers. Miss Quaver the pianist huffed and puffed until I finally found the music stuffed under Miss Lilly's handbag. Imagine! The next day Miss Lilly was humming a silly song and didn't look where she was going.

'Zooot!' she shrieked, as she toppled over Henry.

'EEEEK!' squeaked Henry (hahaha!).

'I'm so sorry, Henry – I'm in a bit of a tizzy these days,' admitted Miss Lilly.

Then she stared dreamily out of the window and forgot to watch our pliés, which was very annoying because my pliés were definitely tippety-top! At the end of class Miss Lilly blew everyone a kiss and waltzed out of the door.

On the way home Alice and I couldn't stop chattering.

'I know why Miss Lilly is in such a tizzy,' I declared, as we skipped down

Apple Tree Lane swinging our school satchels.

'Is she going on a holiday to Dacovia?' Alice asked excitedly.

'No way,' I replied. 'I bet she has a secret boyfriend . . .'

'Really?' Alice stared at me.

'Really-truly, Alice,' I said, leaping nimbly over some geraniums. 'It's too bad Miss Lilly didn't ask us first, because then her boyfriend would definitely be perfect. But if we do a little spying, we can find out who it is!'

Dear Diary

Today Alice and I were brilliant detectives – I think the best in the whole of Mouseland. We sneakily followed Miss Lilly all around the village. We had to squeeze ourselves behind mailboxes, trees and doorways so she wouldn't see us, and we were ever so quiet, except when Alice's tummy rumbled.

'Shhh!' I warned her. 'We're secret detectives now.'

Then I whipped out my pen and wrote everything down.

Angelina's
Special Secret Notebook

<u>10:02 a.m.</u>

Miss Lilly exits ballet school and drops a very large, suspicious-looking letter in the letterbox on the Village Green.

<u>10:11 a.m.</u>

Miss Lilly goes into The Town Mouse, which is the fanciest shop in all of Chipping Cheddar. Miss Lilly stays for ages, and tries on lots of different fancy outfits and all sorts of scarves and pretty things. Miss Lilly finally comes out with three ginormous bags.

<u>11:14 a.m.</u>

Miss Lilly peers in Perfect Paws' window, the snootiest shoe and glove shop in Chipping Cheddar. Miss Lilly goes in and says she needs some 'very special shoes for a very big event'. Then Miss Lilly buys the most expensive shoes in the shop!

<u>12:02 p.m.</u>

Miss Lilly enters the Pink Peppermint Tea Parlour and has a long chat with Mrs Tinsel about party cakes. 'Can you make a fabulous strawberry cheesecake big enough for hundreds of guests?' Miss Lilly asks.

('OOOH!' squeaked Alice, and I had to drag her quickly away.)

Dear Diary

Today Alice and I were very sneaky again.

After our ballet lessons Miss Lilly's telephone rang. She rushed to answer it, and she looked VERY happy.

'Please come immediately,' she said. 'My lessons are over.'

I winked at Alice. What could be more
suspicious than that?

'Let's wait and see who it is,' I
whispered to Alice in the changing room.
Those icky twins Priscilla and Penelope
Pinkpaws almost tripped over each other
trying to listen in (but this little secret
was definitely for Alice's furry ears only!).

We said goodbye to Miss Lilly, but,
instead of going home, we scrambled
behind the hedge outside the ballet
school. Alice clutched her tummy.

'I'm starving,' she complained.

'Shhh! I've got some scrummy liquorice mouse-tails at home,' I whispered. 'But you mustn't make a SQUEAK now!' It wasn't totally true about the liquorice mouse-tails, but at least Alice stopped squeaking. 'Look, here he comes!'

Alice and I stared with wide eyes as a tall figure in a stripy suit trotted up to Miss Lilly's door with a satin box. He rang the bell and twisted his moustache nervously. Alice poked me in the ribs.

'That's Mr Topknot from Topknot's Hat Shop,' she whispered.

'Perfect for Miss Lilly,' I replied. 'He's got grey whiskers and he's still not married.'

The door opened and Miss Lilly stepped out with a huge smile.

'What a pleasure to see you,' she greeted Mr Topknot sweetly. (Oooh, I was soooo right about Miss Lilly!)

Just then Alice's tummy rumbled horribly. Miss Lilly peered into the hedge and spied our two little tails sticking out.

Ooops.

'Hello, Miss Lilly,' we said, as she stared at us in surprise.

'What are you two mouselings up to?' Miss Lilly asked in a very stern voice.

'We were just tidying up your garden for you,' I answered politely, holding up a twig. Miss Lilly raised her eyebrows in disbelief. It was definitely time for Alice and me to be detectives somewhere else.

'Bye, Miss Lilly,' we shouted, as we scampered off across the village green.

Dear Diary

Alice and I spent all Saturday morning in the Treetop Clubhouse chattering about Miss Lilly's secret engagement.

'Just think, we can be sparkly bridesmaids at her wedding,' I told Alice. 'It will be like my dream come true . . .'

Alice and I got soooo excited about Miss Lilly and Mr Topknot that we collected all our pennies and raced off to Miss Fidget's Fantastic Flower Shop. Miss Fidget absolutely detests little

mouselings, but she has the prettiest
flowers in all of Chipping Cheddar and we
definitely wanted the very best for Miss
Lilly.

'A ginormous bouquet, please,' I said,
reaching up on my tippy-toes to plonk our
money down on the counter.

'Too expensive for silly little
mouselings,' said Miss Fidget, peering
down her skinny nose at me.

'We've saved all our pocket money . . .'
I persisted.

'Humph,' Miss Fidget snorted, as she
counted the pennies.

'These are on special offer,' she said
icily, as she shoved a bunch of droopy
daisies across the counter.

Mum always says it's best not to argue
with bad-tempered rodents so, because I
am such a well-behaved mouseling, I

sweetly took the daisies from Miss
Fidget. Then I grabbed Alice and we
raced as fast as our paws could carry us
down to the village green.

I proudly rang Miss Lilly's doorbell.

'Gracious me!' said Miss Lilly, when she
opened the door. 'What's this?'

'CONGRATULATIONS!' we shouted.
Alice and I did our very best curtsies and
presented Miss Lilly with the droopy
bouquet.

'Darlinks, this is very kind,' said Miss
Lilly, 'but what is the occasion?'

'YOUR ENGAGEMENT!' we continued,
shouting even louder.

Miss Lilly scratched her head and
looked really-truly fuddled.

'TO MR TOPKNOT!' I added, in case
she'd forgotten.

Miss Lilly burst out laughing (which was
quite strange).

'Darlinks, I have some explaining to do,'
she said, and she invited us inside.

Dear Diary

Miss Lilly's cottage is always warm and
welcoming, with a cosy fire, a comfy sofa,
and gorgeous photos of Miss Lilly twirling
with the Royal Mouseland Ballet all over
the walls.

'I'm afraid you've made a mistake,' said

Miss Lilly, as she poured hot chocolate into china cups and put a plate of warm cheesy scones and currant buns on the table. 'I have absolutely no intention of marrying Mr Topknot.'

My whiskers trembled and I couldn't even nibble a single scone. 'But what about all those fancy clothes you bought at the Town Mouse shop?' I blurted out. 'And those gorgeous matching shoes and gloves from Perfect Paws?'

Miss Lilly looked surprised. Ooops. I forgot that Alice and I had discovered this in secret!

'You're a good detective, Angelina,' Miss Lilly said, 'but you shouldn't spy.'

'I'm sorry, Miss Lilly,' I mumbled, as a tiny tear trickled down my nose.

'Tut tut. I'll solve the mystery for you,' continued Miss Lilly. Then she opened Mr Topknot's box and pulled out a gorgeous silk hat covered in all sorts of fluffy feathers.

'Oooh . . .' Alice and I sighed, as Miss Lilly showed off her new hat.

'In fact, I bought this hat for the wedding of a famous friend of mine,' she explained.

'Serena Silvertail!' I gasped.

'How did you know, my darlink?' asked Miss Lilly.

'I dreamt it,' I said, remembering the gorgeous bride in the rose garden.

Miss Lilly smiled. 'Yes, Serena Silvertail is marrying Yakov Whiskerovski,' she said.

'The biggest star in the Dacovian Ballet!' I squealed.

Alice whistled and toppled off her chair.

'Yes,' agreed Miss Lilly. 'And they're planning a fabulous wedding at Mouseland Manor.'

Alice scrambled back on her chair and sighed. 'Think of all the gorgeous food and cake . . .' she said dreamily.

'Now you know why I've been busy shopping,' continued Miss Lilly, patting me on the head. 'I must look my best for such an important wedding.'

I gazed longingly at Miss Lilly's fancy hat, and wished that I could go to Serena

Silvertail's wedding too. I knew I would have to be really-truly brave about not being Miss Lilly's bridesmaid now, but I couldn't help feeling horribly sad.

Dear Diary

Even though Miss Lilly's not-getting-married was the worst news ever, I managed to take a few sips of hot chocolate and nibble three scones for extra strength (before Alice gobbled up absolutely everything!).

'Thank you for a lovely visit,' I said to Miss Lilly, when there wasn't a single crumb left on our plates.

'You're very welcome, darlinks,' said Miss Lilly. 'Now, no more spying.'

Just then we heard car brakes screeching outside, and Miss Lilly peered out of the window.

'Goodness me. It's Serena Silvertail!'
she gasped, opening the door.

   Serena Silvertail burst into the cottage
with wild eyes.

   'Save me, Lilly!' she cried, throwing
herself into Miss Lilly's arms.

   'My dear Serena,' said Miss Lilly.
'Whatever is the matter?'

Alice and I stared. Could this really be the sparkly ballerina on our *Cindermouse* poster?

'My wedding is a complete disaster!' sobbed Miss Silvertail.

Miss Lilly sent us off to make a cup of tea in the kitchen while she helped poor Serena Silvertail on to the sofa.

'I must rehearse day and night for my next big Royal Ballet performance,' sobbed Serena Silvertail, 'so there's no wedding dress, no flowers, no bridesmaids. Yakov is furious. The wedding is off!'

Alice and I brought Serena Silvertail a cup of elderflower tea, and she gulped it down. I noticed that even though she seemed the most unhappy bride ever, Serena Silvertail was wearing a truly ginormous diamond ring.

'Don't worry about a thing, my darlink,'
said Miss Lilly kindly. 'I'll help make your
wedding day perfect.'

Serena Silvertail looked up with weepy
eyes, and pulled a very long roll of
scribbly paper out of her bag.

'Here's my list,' she said, handing it over.

'Goodness gracious . . .' said Miss Lilly,
staring in horror.

I looked over Miss Lilly's shoulder, my whiskers twitching with excitement. Serena Silvertail definitely needed lots of help – and so did Miss Lilly. I poked Alice in the ribs and smiled ever so sweetly at Serena Silvertail.

'Alice and I could be your helpers too,' I said, and Alice nodded happily.

'Can you run very fast and do all my errands?' Serena Silvertail asked us.

'Definitely,' we agreed.

'Can you find a brilliant seamstress for my dress?' cried Serena Silvertail.

'My mum can sew anything!' I boasted.

'And what about bridesmaids?' Serena Silvertail continued, sniffling away.

This was it! Maybe my dream of being a bridesmaid could really-truly come true!!!

'Well . . . Alice and I could be your

bridesmaids,' I said, holding my breath and crossing my paws behind my back for good luck. Serena Silvertail peered thoughtfully at us.

'What a charming idea – two little bridesmaids,' she said at last, looking brighter.

'YIPPEE!' I shouted.

Alice and I couldn't stop squeaking as we danced in circles around and around Miss Lilly's sitting room. We were going to be the best bridesmaids ever!

Dear Diary

My mum's tail shot up in surprise when I told her that Alice and I were going to be the bridesmaids at Serena Silvertail's wedding.

'Imagine that,' she said, smiling at us.

'And you'll be very busy sewing,' I said,

'because Serena Silvertail wants you to make her wedding dress.'

'What an honour,' said Mum, raising her eyebrows. I could tell that Mum was secretly VERY pleased that I had been such a clever mouseling and found her such an important job sewing Serena Silvertail's wedding dress.

'Polly be a bride-maid too?' begged Polly, banging her cup.

'You'll have to wait until you're big like me,' I explained.

Then I spied my silly little cousin Henry hiding under the table.

'WILLIAM AND I WILL BE THE BOY BRIDESMAIDS,' he squeaked, popping up.

'That's ridiculous!' I shouted.

'I'm sure Miss Lilly will be delighted to have more helpers,' said Mum, picking up the phone to call my ballet teacher. I could hardly believe my furry ears when Mum told me Miss Lilly had agreed! I rushed out of the door to tell Alice the terrible news. Of course, Alice was truly horrified, so we raced off together to Mrs Thimble's shop for liquorice mouse-tails to make us feel better.

Mrs Thimble's shop was packed with customers chattering about Serena Silvertail's wedding. Everyone in Chipping Cheddar has heard about it. Mrs Thimble told us that tons of famous dancers and actors are invited, and guess what? The *Mouseland Gazette* will publish a huge story all about it – and my dad is the reporter.

Everything would be perfect if only my silly cousin Henry and William Longtail weren't invited. Every time I think of

those two pests my whiskers start
twitching madly.

'It's NOT fair!' I complained at supper.
  'I'm sure the boys will be on their best
behaviour,' said Mum.

  'And you'll be busy waltzing with me,'
said Dad proudly.
  'Thanks, Dad,' I said, still sulking a bit.

But then I had a most brilliant idea. It was about a very special performance . . .

Dear Diary

I phoned Alice as soon as I woke up this morning.

'Treetop Club Top-secret Meeting,' I whispered.

'Wait for me!' Alice yelped. And in a flick of a mouse-tail later she was scrambling up the ladder.

'We need to give Serena Silvertail a fantabulous wedding present,' I announced.

'What about a nice box of chocolates?' asked Alice, licking her lips.

'Even more fantabulous than that,' I replied. 'We're going to perform a special ballet for her.'

'Just you and me?' asked Alice.

'Definitely. There will be absolutely NO BOY mouselings!' I said. (Ugh. I didn't want silly William and Henry spoiling things!)

'It will be a special bridesmaid ballet.'

'Will Miss Lilly help us?' asked Alice, searching for nibbles.

'No way – it has to be a secret,' I told her, opening our Secret Sweetie Box.

'But we might get mixed up . . .' said Alice, handing out Cheddar creams.

'Don't be such a worry-mouse,' I said.

Just then I remembered we'd promised to help Miss Lilly every day. 'Ooops. Alice, we're supposed to be at Miss Lilly's right now!'

When we arrived at Miss Lilly's cottage, she was busily writing more lists and talking on the phone at the same time. She definitely looked frazzled (Mum says it isn't good manners to tell grown-ups when they look frazzled, how weird is that?).

'Off you go,' Miss Lilly said, handing me her scribbles. Alice and I felt ever so important as we trotted around the village doing special wedding errands. But can you believe it? Everywhere we went, my annoying little cousin Henry trailed along behind us with silly William

Longtail. (I simply HATE boy mouselings!)

'WE'RE WEDDING HELPERS TOO, ANGELINA,' Henry squeaked, hopping beside me.

'You are not, Henry,' I said, glaring at him.

'Actually, we're Serena Silvertail's pageboys,' bragged William, smiling cheekily at me. Alice and I skipped away as fast as we could, but those two pests kept following us.

Our first stop was Pawprints's Print Shop. Mr Pawprints proudly showed us his fanciest wedding invitation designs, and I picked out a really bright pinky-pink one, because pink is my tip-top FAVOURITE colour. Mr Pawprints said it was a brilliant choice, but then he showed me a plain white design. 'Perhaps Serena Silvertail

would like something more traditional?' he
asked.

'Hmmm . . . No, definitely the pink
ones,' I decided.

'Serena Silvertail is ordering two
hundred pinky-pink invitations,' I said,
feeling very grown up. I smiled at Alice
and completely ignored the two naughty
mouselings peeping over her shoulder.
Grrrr . . .

Our next stop was Fidget's Fantastic Flower Shop. Henry and William followed us inside, giggling all the way. Can you imagine? Those two silly-billies wiggled their ears and stuck out their tongues all the time I was ordering the gorgeous wedding roses. Miss Fidget grumbled and shook her paws at them. 'I'll report you two ruffians to Constable Crumble,' she warned. That did the trick. Before I could count ten whiskers, those naughty mouselings scampered off with their tails between their paws.

Dear Diary

Miss Lilly has tons of new errands for us every day, and she dashes off to Mouseland Manor whenever she's not teaching ballet. It's not so easy-peasy to get everything ready for such a big fancy wedding, and bridesmaids can get quite frazzled too – even the very bestest bridesmaids like us!

Alice and I already have sore paws from trudging all over Chipping Cheddar. We deliver messages and collect packages all day long, and we mustn't forget to stop by The Beauty Mouse Spa and reserve fancy paw manicures, tail massages and fur highlights for Serena Silvertail – she absolutely can't live without them!

Alice moans a lot because we can't stop for yummy snacks any more, and we hardly have time to sneak off to our comfy clubhouse either. Even Mum says she's never been so frazzled. Our little cottage is crammed with silks and fabrics,

ribbons, beads and sewing boxes. Dad
sighs and complains because he can't sit
down anywhere, and Polly drives Mum mad
dressing up in all the fancy sewing stuff
(although I have to admit she sometimes
looks kind of cute).

When the phone started ringing at
breakfast this morning, Mum's tail
definitely drooped.

'Is the wedding dress ready yet?'
Serena Silvertail asked for the hundredth
time. Mum had to stop everything to talk
while the toast burned and the milk
boiled over. (Polly and I are VERY fed up
with burnt toast for breakfast!)

'WAAAAA!' shrieked Polly, banging her
cup.

'Crumbs,' sighed Mum, staring at the
mess.

Dear Diary

Alice and I are the busiest mouselings ever – it turns out that bridesmaids have to do absolutely EVERYTHING for the bride! How unfair is that? We're busy hopping all over Chipping Cheddar every day and then we have to sneak off to secretly rehearse our Bridesmaid Ballet. Even Alice, who is almost ALWAYS a cheerful mouseling, is getting her whiskers in a twist during rehearsals.

Today was definitely our worst rehearsal ever. 'Remember, I'm the star and you're my partner,' I told her. 'At the end of the ballet I'll leap into your arms and you hold me up.'

'Yikes,' said Alice, looking a bit nervous (as if I'm soooo heavy!).

I twirled towards Alice and performed a graceful grand jeté, but she toppled over and we both crashed into Mum's flower bed. (Ooops. Mum won't be too happy about that.)

'Oooh,' complained Alice, picking herself up.

'Practice makes perfect,' I reminded her, because ballerinas never give up when they fall down. Even if they do have to scrape some flower-bed mud off their tutus.

I twirled towards Alice again, but instead of catching me in her paws, Alice turned round and trotted off towards the kitchen.

'Well, practice makes my tummy rumble,' she complained.

Dear Diary

Today Mr Pawprints finished the gorgeous pinky-pink wedding invitations that I had

chosen. Miss Lilly looked at them with wide
eyes and said they were 'most original'.
(I'm sure this is a very big compliment.)
Here's what the invitations say:

Miss Serena Silvertail

and Mr Yakov Whiskerovski

request the pleasure of your company

at their wedding in the rose gardens

on 22 June

followed by dinner and dancing.

The Mouseland Manor

Chipping Cheddar

Boltholes

Mouseland

Isn't that the most romantic thing since
Swiss cheese? After we put all the

stamps on, Alice and I spent all afternoon
rushing to the post office and stuffing
tons of the invitations into the post box.

Dear Diary

Alice and I have been absolutely dying to visit Mouseland Manor and today we had a truly BIG surprise. Imagine – Yakov Whiskerovski zoomed into Chipping Cheddar in his yellow Mouserati to specially invite us! Serena Silvertail sat beside him in a silk scarf and dark glasses, waving to everyone just like a film star. She is soooo glamorous. The Mouserati screeched to a stop outside Miss Lilly's cottage and my whiskers tingled with excitement – but then Henry and William raced round the corner and jumped in beside Serena Silvertail. Horrors!

'Humph,' I grumbled to Alice. 'What a nerve!'

'I CAN'T WAIT TO SEE MOUSELAND MANOR,' squeaked my cheeky little cousin. I was sure Serena Silvertail would tell Henry off, but she smiled and tweaked his whiskers. Grrrr . . .

Alice and I had to squeeze into Miss Lilly's shabby little mousemobile and we bumped along in the dust behind the gleaming Mouserati as it roared off through the countryside with Henry and William laughing their silly heads off.

Mouseland Manor is almost as big as the royal palace, and just as fantabulous. The lobby is gleaming gold, and fancy couples were chattering together in the swanky restaurant and lounging around the pool while waiters brought them luscious drinks and snacks (which definitely made Alice's tummy rumble).

'This is more like it,' I said to Alice, as I gazed at the golden doors and imagined myself twirling through the rose garden in my bridesmaid dress.

A uniformed doormouse rushed to help Yakov Whiskerovski and Serena Silvertail out of the Mouserati, and a pencil-thin hostess in a snappy suit stepped forward to greet them.

'Welcome to Mouseland Manor,' she said, extending a silky paw. 'Madame Snootfur, at your service.'

'HELLO, MY NAME IS HENRY,' my little cousin squeaked politely, but Madame Snootfur just sniffed at him and turned away.

Yakov Whiskerovski twitched his whiskers nervously.

'Where's the Grand Ballroom?' he asked. 'We must have dancing!'

I nudged Alice. 'See?' I whispered. Everyone was definitely going to love our surprise bridesmaid ballet dance!

Henry and William dashed off ahead,

while Madame Snootfur led us to the
Grand Ballroom with her nose in the air.
Then she nattered on for absolutely ages
about pink champagne and orchestras and
silver goblets and all that fancy wedding
stuff. Alice pointed excitedly to all the
chandeliers.

'Have you ever seen such a ginormous
ballroom?' she asked.
'Perfect for our ballet,' I said,

imagining all the guests clapping and cheering for us.

Alice wriggled her nose doubtfully as we watched Henry and William marching across the ballroom behind Yakov Whiskerovski, trying to be perfect pageboys. How gruesome!

'Won't it be scary, dancing at the wedding, Angelina?' asked Alice.

'Don't worry,' I assured her. 'Just follow me. We'll leap onstage with the orchestra just like this –' Then I twirled brilliantly across the Grand Ballroom and bounded into a spectacular grand jeté.

'WATCH OUT, ANGELINA!' squeaked Henry.

Dear Diary

After I crashed into the Mouseland Manor buffet table, Miss Lilly rushed me off to see Dr Tuttle. I guess my grand jeté was a bit too grand. I landed upside down on top of a ginormous strawberry cheesecake and got a terrible bump on my nose. Alice said I looked like a special party pudding all covered in strawberries and cream (but she didn't giggle because she is my very bestest friend). Henry and William stared goggle-eyed while that horrid Madame Snootfur glared at me with quivering whiskers.

'Wow, that was some leap,' said William.

'The Grand Ballroom is not a playground,' grumbled Miss Snootfur.

Miss Lilly and Serena Silvertail peered carefully at my nose.

'Where does it hurt?' asked Miss Lilly.

'OUCH!' I yelped.

'Little bridesmaids should look before they leap,' joked Serena Silvertail

(hahaha), while Yakov Whiskerovski
scowled at the squashed cheesecake.

'Perhaps you need a new bridesmaid,' he
said.

Yakov Whiskerovski's horrible words
squished my heart into tiny bits and I
sobbed all the way to Dr Tuttle's office.
When we arrived I tried to be brave
even though I was really-truly miserable.

'I was just practising a grand jeté,' I explained, while Dr Tuttle examined my bump.

'You little ballerinas are tougher than footballers,' Dr Tuttle chuckled. Then he wrapped tons of white bandages around my poor purple nose.

On the way home Henry scrambled in next to me.

'YOU'RE A VERY BRAVE MOUSELING,

ANGELINA,' he squeaked (sometimes my little cousin can actually be quite intelligent).

Dear Diary

Ballerinas are absolutely always professional. Even though I have a terrible purple nose bump, I've been practising the Bridesmaid Ballet every day with Alice (after she made me promise not to do any more grand jetés). Luckily, Serena Silvertail said I could still be her bridesmaid. YIPPEE!

'Don't worry about Yakov,' she added, giving me a hug. 'He can be rather temperamental.'

Alice whispered in my ear, 'That Yakov Whiskerovski may be a tippety-top dancer, but he's not a specially kind sort of mouse like Serena Silvertail.'

'He's definitely not very fond of a silly-billy mouseling like me,' I replied with a sigh. For the first time I was getting a teeny tiny bit nervous. What if Yakov Whiskerovski gets temperamental about the Bridesmaid Ballet?

Dear Diary

Today is my lucky day. This morning Dr Tuttle took most of the bandages off and my nose bump is definitely not so gruesomely purple and sore any more. I did NOT want to perform our ballet with my nose wrapped up like a mummy – imagine!

The other big news is that soon we'll have our new dresses. Peach is Serena Silvertail's tip-top favourite colour (although secretly I think pinky-pink would be MUCH nicer!) so Alice and I agreed on some silky peachy fabric for our dresses. My mum has been sewing madly for days. Alice and I can hardly wait! Serena Silvertail invited us to go shopping at Perfect Paws for our sparkly wedding slippers and rose flower baskets. And guess what? My cousin Henry and William Longtail were already there, grinning at themselves in the mirror. They were spruced up in bright blue pageboy outfits. Henry's fur was brushed and fluffy and even his whiskers were shiny – he was so clean I hardly recognized him!

'Don't my pageboys look handsome?' asked Serena Silvertail.

Alice and I giggled. They're only silly-billy BOYS after all!

After we finished shopping, Alice and I waved goodbye to Serena Silvertail and skipped home together.

'Aren't we the luckiest mouselings?' asked Alice.

'The luckiest in all of Mouseland,' I agreed, thinking about being gorgeous bridesmaids in our own special ballet . . .

Dear Diary

Today Serena Silvertail came specially
to Honeysuckle Cottage after her
rehearsals to try on her wedding dress.
Because Alice and I are very responsible
mouselings (and also because Mum
told us we had to) we played
'bridesmaids' with Polly in the sitting
room while Mum helped Serena
Silvertail get ready.

Finally, Serena Silvertail appeared in
her fantabulous dress and gauzy veil, and
she looked even prettier than my dream
bride. Alice and I rushed upstairs and
changed into our peachy bridesmaid
dresses so Serena Silvertail could see
how gorgeous we were too.

Of course, as soon as my sister Polly
spied my new dress and slippers, she had
a terrible tantrum.

'Polly want sparkle shoes!' she wailed.
'Polly want to be a bride-maid!'

'Don't cry pet,' said Mum soothingly.
'I'm sure Serena Silvertail would love to
have a tiny bridesmaid.'

'That's not fair, Mum!' I shouted. 'Polly
is WAY too little to be a bridesmaid!'

'She's such a little darling,' said Serena Silvertail, as tiny tears dripped off Polly's whiskers (totally on purpose!). 'Polly can help scatter the rose petals.'

Noooo! How could Serena Silvertail be so horrid?

'Me throw petals,' declared Polly, giggling with delight.

'And you'll help your little sister, Angelina,' said Mum sternly.

I was so upset I stomped up to my room and cried buckets. Now I'm definitely the saddest mouseling in all of Mouseland . . .

Dear Diary

Why are some days soooo miserable?

I had to go with Mum and Polly to Furball's Fabric Emporium today because

Serena Silvertail wants Polly to have a bridesmaid dress just like mine. How gruesome is that? And Polly has to have matching sparkly peach slippers too, and her own little rose basket. She is such a copymouse!

But when we got there Polly wouldn't stand still for a moment. She scrambled away to play hide-and-seek all over Mr Furball's shop and poor Mum had to chase after her. Then my naughty baby sister threw herself on the floor in one of her terrible tantrums.

'WAAAAA!' she screeched.

'What a simply revolting noise,' said a familiar snooty voice.

It was Mrs Pinkpaws with Priscilla and Penelope. They stared at Polly as if she was the most disgusting little rat ever.

'Please excuse this dreadful

disturbance,' Mr Furball apologized.

'Angelina's little sister is such a menace,' said Priscilla, wrinkling her nose.

'Babies like her shouldn't be allowed out,' agreed Penelope.

(Ugh. Aren't those Pinkpaws the most horrid mouselings ever?)

Poor Mum's whiskers were trembling as she paid the bill. I picked up howling Polly and gave her a cheesy mint from my pocket.

'My daughters were always such sweet babies,' said Mrs Pinkpaws, eyeing Polly coldly.

'But they're definitely NOT sweet now!' I replied.

Mrs Pinkpaws gasped, and Priscilla and Penelope stuck their tongues out at me, but I just smiled as Polly and I twirled out of Furball's Fabric Emporium.

Dear Diary

Can you believe it? Serena Silvertail's wedding is next week and even I am getting in a tizzy now because the Bridesmaid Ballet has to be perfect (and at the moment it is definitely NOT).

Everyone in the village is madly getting ready for all the fancy guests to arrive. The Old Goat's Cheese Inn has a bright new coat of paint, and Miss Fidget has put pots of white lilies all along the high street. Mum finally finished sewing a tiny bridesmaid outfit for Polly. I have to admit that my sister does look very sweet all dressed up, but it's hard to stop her splashing in mud puddles!

Miss Lilly gave a bridal shower party for Serena Silvertail, and her little cottage was bursting with guests. Everyone from Mrs Thimble to Mr Bell the old postman was invited. Henry and William and Alice and I went early to help set out all the yummy food (greedy Alice ate tons even before the guests arrived). There was purple passion flower punch, along with Mrs Tinsel's pretty sugar hearts, strawberry jam tarts and Cheddar fudge cake specially baked for the party. Scrumptious!

'Remember, no grand jetés on the table, Angelina, darlink,' Miss Lilly joked.

Hahaha.

'I hope Mrs Tinsel makes tons of this yummy cake for the wedding,' said Alice, gobbling her third huge piece.

Dear Diary

Today, Serena Silvertail and Yakov Whiskerovski had a gruesome fight about the wedding music. Serena Silvertail said she wanted a lovely piano and romantic violins, but Yakov Whiskerovski insisted on loud drums, trumpets and cymbals. Finally, Yakov Whiskerovski slammed the door and stomped off in a temper, and Serena Silvertail collapsed sobbing on the sofa (again!).

'What a silly-billy thing to fight about,' Alice whispered.

'I know,' I said, 'grown-ups act so weird sometimes.'

Secretly, my tummy was feeling quite gruesome as I imagined all the nasty things grumpy Yakov Whiskerovski would say about our surprise ballet. Gulp!

Miss Lilly sighed and gave Serena Silvertail a hug.

'I'm sure he didn't mean to upset you,' Miss Lilly said kindly.

'How can I marry such a revolting rodent?' wailed Serena Silvertail.

A few minutes later the doorbell rang, and William staggered into the cottage carrying a ginormous bouquet of peachy roses.

'Special delivery from Fidget's Fantastic Flower Shop,' William said, 'with a card for Serena Silvertail.'

Serena Silvertail dried her eyes on her

hanky and read the pretty card.

'Darling Yakov has changed his mind and now he agrees with me about the piano and violins,' she said, smelling the roses. 'Isn't he adorable?'

'I guess they're getting married after all,' Alice whispered in my ear.

Dear Diary

Today is the Big Wedding Day!
Alice and I arrived at the wedding just like two fairy princesses, along with

Henry and William in their blue pageboy suits and neatly trimmed fur. William's dad, Mr Longtail, was our special chauffeur and drove us in a gleaming white mousemobile. We all sat up very straight next to Serena Silvertail in her elegant wedding dress and diamond necklace and earrings – she was definitely sparkling!

Crowds were waving and cheering along the streets, and Serena Silvertail smiled at everyone while Alice and I smoothed her dress and held her bouquet. In our special bridesmaid dresses, with crowns of tiny pink rosebuds around our ears, we were definitely the prettiest bridesmaids ever! William Longtail couldn't stop grinning, and Henry kept squeaking, 'YOU LOOK SO PRETTY, ANGELINA.'

When the limousine arrived at Mouseland

Manor, Alice and I stepped out gracefully
and lifted Serena Silvertail's delicate veil.
We held our heads up high and we didn't
wiggle a whisker! All the fancy guests were
seated in the rose garden waiting for the
wedding to begin, and Serena Silvertail
looked around nervously.

'Is everyone ready?' she asked.
'Polly's feeling a bit shy . . .' said Mum,
holding Polly's paw.

I gave Polly a hug and whispered in her ear, 'Remember you're a big girl like me today.'

'A big special girl,' Polly agreed.

'You're big enough to help me throw rose petals,' I continued.

'PETALS!' shouted Polly. (Sometimes I am definitely a very responsible older sister.)

The violins began to play, and Polly trotted off beside me, happily tossing rose petals in the air. Henry and William marched along smartly together, while Alice and I did our best to be especially dainty. We carried the bride's veil with one paw and tossed petals in the air with the other – and when Alice tripped on her hem and tore her dress we paid almost absolutely no attention.

'Rats!' said Alice, but she kept on tossing lots of petals.

Yakov Whiskerovski was waiting under the arch of white roses. When he saw Serena Silvertail coming through the garden in her lovely wedding gown, he couldn't stop staring.

'At least Yakov Whiskerovski isn't being horrid on his wedding day,' I whispered to Alice. We sat down for the ceremony and didn't twitch a whisker (except when Serena Silvertail said 'I do' and kissed

Yakov Whiskerovski smack on the lips, which really made us giggle!).

After the wedding ceremony, all the gorgeous guests rushed off to the Grand Ballroom for dinner and dancing. Alice gazed at all the scrumptious food on the buffet and her tail twitched madly.

'I'm going to taste absolutely everything,' she said happily.

But my tummy wasn't rumbling at all – I was far too frazzled to nibble a thing. All I could think about was our surprise ballet. I wondered if it was too late to hide under the table! Everyone else was hungry though, and the dinner lasted for AGES.

When the last slice of Pink Passion wedding cake was all gobbled up, I knew our big moment had come. I told myself that I was not a scaredy-mouse, and I

poked Alice in the ribs. We stood up
bravely together in front of the crowd.

'As a special surprise for the bride and
groom,' I announced, 'Alice Nimbletoes and
I will now perform the Bridesmaid Ballet.'

Miss Lilly stared in amazement as Alice
and I curtsied to the wedding couple, and
Mum and Dad looked nervously at each
other as we skipped on to the stage. But
they didn't have to worry one bit, because
Alice and I remembered our dance
perfectly!

We twirled around the stage just like two ballet bridesmaids getting ready for the biggest wedding ever. We danced as if we were skipping through Chipping Cheddar visiting all our favourite shops and doing our special errands. We twirled as we 'ooohed' and 'aaahed' over wedding flowers and invitations, and then we leapt across the stage and pretended we were nibbling liquorice mouse-tails at Mrs Thimble's Shop. Next we pretended we were skipping across the village green and peering into the windows at Topknot's Hat Shop and Perfect Paws. Finally, we danced as if we were prancing around the rose garden behind the bride – just like the real wedding! In fact, everything went brilliantly right up until it was time to do my fantabulous grand jeté. Then Alice's tail began to droop.

'Come on, Alice,' I whispered. 'I need you to catch me!'

At that very moment Yakov Whiskerovski jumped out of his chair.

'Uh-oh,' I whispered. 'We're in BIG trouble now.'

In one bound, Yakov Whiskerovski leapt on to the stage and stood beside us. Alice and I tried to scurry away, but he quickly caught us by our tails!

'I have come to join your dance,' he announced with a bow.

Alice and I could not believe our furry ears. Yakov Whiskerovski is always so horrible and temperamental. How could he be acting just like Prince Charming now? Then Yakov Whiskerovski smiled and took our little paws in his big paws and we waltzed across the stage together – just the three of us. Miss Lilly stared at us goggle-eyed as Alice and I gracefully pirouetted with the Dacovia Ballet's most famous dancer.

'And now for our grand finale,' said Yakov Whiskerovski. He winked at me and I twirled faster and faster before doing a truly spectacular grand jeté way up into the air. Yakov Whiskerovski caught me in his arms and lifted me up just like a feather. Cameras flashed, and for a

moment I was really truly the most
brilliant ballerina in all of Mouseland.

Dear Diary

Today Chipping Cheddar seemed soooo
quiet – and all the streets were empty.
Henry, William, Alice and I helped Miss
Lilly pack tons of gifts and luggage into
the yellow Mouserati for the newly-weds,
and then we all said goodbye.

'We'll be back soon,' said Serena Silvertail, who was now the new Mrs Whiskerovski!

'And we'll do another ballet,' promised Yakov Whiskerovski with a wink.

Then the happy couple waved goodbye to us and zoomed off in their Mouserati.

'HAPPY HONEYMOON!' we shouted as we watched them disappear.

Miss Lilly turned around with a big smile.

'I have a nice surprise for you,' she said.

We skipped across the village green to Miss Lilly's cosy cottage and snuggled on her sofa with cups of hot chocolate and cheesy nutcake.

'You're on the front page,' said Miss Lilly, and she showed us the *Mouseland*

Gazette. There I was, way up in the air with Yakov Whiskerovski. Imagine!

I read the headline out loud: '"Chipping Cheddar Ballerinas Dance with Stars".'

'Oooh,' said Alice, rolling her eyes. 'So now we're stars too!'

And that gave me a most brilliant idea.

'Let's go, Alice,' I said as I dashed outside. Alice raced after me, and we did fantabulous grand jetés and pirouettes all across the village green just like star ballerinas – because practice definitely makes perfect!